PUFFIN BOOKS

NIGHTMARE BEFORE CHRISTMAS

'Year after year, it's the same routine,' he
told his little ghost dog, Zero, who floated
alongside him, his jack-o'-lantern nose
gleaming. 'Terror. Shock. Shrieks and
moans. I scare the bravest of the brave.
But I've grown so weary of the sound of
screams, Zero. They leave me cold. I can't
help but wonder why I bother at all.' Jack
sighed heavily. 'I'm sick and tired of
scaring everyone. I want to do something
. . . different.

TIM BURTON'S NIGHTMARE BEFORE CHRISTMAS

A Novel by Daphne Skinner
Based on the Motion Picture from Touchstone Pictures
Screenplay by Caroline Thompson
Story by Tim Burton, Michael McDowell and Caroline Thompson
Produced by Tim Burton and Denise Di Novi
Directed by Henry Selick

PUFFIN BOOKS

PUFFIN BOOKS

Published by the Penguin Group
Penguin Books Ltd, 27 Wrights Lane, London W8 5TZ, England
Penguin Books USA Inc., 375 Hudson Street, New York, New York 10014, USA
Penguin Books Australia Ltd, Ringwood, Victoria, Australia
Penguin Books Canada Ltd, 10 Alcorn Avenue, Toronto, Ontario, Canada M4V 3B2
Penguin Books (NZ) Ltd, 182–190 Wairau Road, Auckland 10, New Zealand

Penguin Books Ltd, Registered Offices: Hardmondsworth, Middlesex, England

First published by Hyperion Books for Children 1993
Published in Puffin Books 1994
3 5 7 9 10 8 6 4 2

Puffin Film and TV Tie-in edition first published 1994

Filmset in Great Britain by Goodfellow & Egan

Made and printed in Great Britain by Clays Ltd, St Ives plc

Under the orange disc of the moon, in a place called Hallowe'enland, the creatures of the night were busy. Grinning jack-o'-lanterns danced in the graveyard. Werewolves howled. Corpses, vampires and witches joined their voices in a ghoulish chorus of glee. Tonight was their favourite night of all – Hallowe'en!

And it had been a splendid one. As they gathered down in the centre of town to celebrate, everyone agreed on that. They also agreed that such a night would not have been possible without the help of their leader, the king of Hallowe'en, Jack Skellington.

Everyone cheered wildly as Jack stepped into the town square.

'You were a scream, Jack,' called a vampire.

'It was terrifying!' added a werewolf.

'You're a witch's fondest dream,' cackled two of Hallowe'enland's gnarliest crones.

They cheered again as the Mayor clapped Jack on his rickety shoulders.

'Thanks, Jack!' boomed the Mayor. 'We owe it all to you! Why, without your leadership –'

Jack cut him off. 'Not at all, Mayor,' he said with a hint of impatience – or was it something else? – in his voice. But the Mayor didn't notice that anything was wrong. He was too intent on keeping the crowd's attention focused where it should be: on himself.

'It's now my pleasure to give out the

wonderful prizes,' he announced. 'Our first award goes to the vampires, for most blood drained in a single evening. Congratulations, Fanged Ones!' he boomed as the audience cheered. 'Second prize,' he went on, 'is to the Dark Lagoon Leeches, who also have a real taste for blood . . .'

The crowd cheered again, and Jack took the opportunity to slip away. It was strange, but all the applause made him feel terrible. He needed to go somewhere that would cheer him up. He headed for the graveyard.

He was so preoccupied that he didn't notice the frail, melancholy figure of Sally the Rag Doll watching him. Sally was sad, too, and with good reason. She had been created by the town's official Evil Scientist. Try as she might, and she had tried many times, Sally couldn't seem to escape from him. Although he was confined to a wheelchair, he guarded her jealously.

Sally sighed and leaned against a tombstone. She had tried to escape tonight, but once again the Evil Scientist had stopped her. Well, he'd almost stopped her. In their struggle Sally had even pulled off one of her own stitched-on arms before getting away and running here, to the graveyard.

An arm was a small price to pay, thought Sally, especially since she was an expert seamstress and could always sew herself back together. She just *had* to get free of the Evil Scientist. But how?

Her unhappy thoughts were interrupted by the sight of Jack Skellington walking along slowly, his bony shoulders hunched and his skull hanging low. Sally couldn't believe her eyes. Jack looked almost . . . sad. But what could he possibly be sad about? He was the pride of Hallowe'enland!

She soon found out. Jack's bony feet carried him so close to where she sat that she could hear every word he uttered. To Sally's astonishment, they were words of woe and weariness, boredom and frustration.

'Year after year, it's the same routine,' he told his little ghost dog, Zero, who floated alongside him, his jack-o'-lantern nose gleaming. 'Terror. Shock. Shrieks and moans. I scare the bravest of the brave. But I've grown so weary of the sound of screams, Zero. They leave me cold. I can't help but wonder why I bother at all.' Jack sighed heavily. 'I'm sick and tired of scaring everyone. I want to do something . . . different.

'But I just don't know what it is,' he told his little dog. 'Why don't I know what it is, Zero? Why?'

Sally's rag-doll heart melted. Jack was suffering, just as she was. She stood up, wanting to reach out to him.

'I know how you feel,' she whispered under her breath, almost hoping he'd hear.

But it was too late. Lost in his sorrow, Jack had gone.

Now a tear rolled down Sally's face. As best as she could with only one arm, she began to pick a bouquet for the Evil Scientist — a bunch of deadly nightshade. With it she would make a powerful sleeping potion. Maybe then she could escape.

CHAPTER TWO

The next day's weather was perfect for Hallowe'enland. The skies were dark and gloomy, and a bone-chilling wind blew restlessly through town. Of course, most people in Hallowe'enland didn't notice the weather. They were asleep. Night was their time.

But the Mayor was awake. He had important things to take care of. At an hour when all good witches and werewolves were dreaming wicked dreams, he was bustling across town in his hearse, with one thing and one thing only on his mind: the plan for next year's Hallowe'en. And for this he needed Jack.

The Mayor stepped out of his hearse at Jack's tower, his arms laden with blueprints, lists and plans. He rang Jack's bell once, then half a dozen times, but got no response.

'Jack!' he called. 'I've got the plans for next year's Hallowe'en! I need to go over them with you, Jack, so we can get started!'

Silence.

'Jack, please!' he called, a note of desperation creeping into his voice. 'I'm only an elected official here. I can't make decisions by myself. I need you, Jack!'

More silence.

The Mayor began to get angry. Like most politicians, he was a two-faced creature. Depending on his mood, his head would swivel from a smile to a frown. Frowning at the moment, he shouted in his most commanding voice, 'Jack! Answer me!' But this didn't work, either. As it slowly dawned on the Mayor that Jack was not at home, a cluster of worries sprang up in his busy brain. Where was Jack? Was he missing? And if he was, what would happen to next year's Hallowe'en?

The surprising truth was that Jack didn't know where he was, either. His mournful meandering had taken him far from Hallowe'enland, miles from anything familiar, into a deep, dark forest. But his gloom was so overpowering that he paid no attention to his surroundings. It wasn't until Zero barked at him impatiently that Jack stopped. Then he looked around in confusion, as if waking from a dream.

'Zero! Where are we?' he asked. The little dog whined. He was lost, too. A soft wind sighed through the trees.

Jack saw that he was in a clearing lit only by the faintest starlight. The enormous trees around him were like none he knew. Doorways were carved into their trunks. And mysterious symbols were carved into the doorways. Jack had never seen anything so strange.

'What *is* this?' he murmured to Zero, examining each tree in turn. One doorway bore the sign of an egg that was decorated with stripes and flowers. Another was carved with a great big heart. A third was carved with a four-leaf clover. But the doorway that truly fascinated Jack bore a tree on its trunk – a tree festooned with decorations and topped with a star. He moved closer.

The doorway rattled on its hinges, as if inviting him to open it. How could he resist?

Jack pulled the door open. For an instant there was only silence. Then a cool gust of wind, like a giant icy hand, wrapped itself around Jack and drew him inside. He screamed in terror, but only Zero heard. Then the door clanged shut, and not even Zero could help.

CHAPTER THREE

Jack's bones stirred. He found himself lying on something cold, yet oddly soft and comforting. His eyes opened. First he saw a night sky sparkling with stars. Then he saw . . . white! It was everywhere, blanketing the ground, the trees, and the houses with its soft glow.

Jack picked up a handful of the stuff. It felt cool and powdery, and it shaped nicely into a ball. What is this? he wondered, throwing the ball into the air and watching it land nearby with a small, satisfying thud. Whatever this stuff was, he liked it! Jack leapt to his feet, suddenly feeling light as a cloud. He couldn't wait to explore.

This town, he realized very quickly, was nothing like Hallowe'enland. People on the streets were singing. Children were throwing balls of the white stuff at each other and laughing. The trees were covered with bright decorations and topped with stars. And inside cosy little houses people sat together – talking, reading, singing – even hugging and kissing! Jack kept walking, enchanted by everything around him.

Before long he noticed something else. He hadn't yet heard a single scream, only laughter and sweet music. The smells wafting towards him through the crisp night air were delicious – cakes and pies, not swamp gas, smoke and witch's brew. And children here, Jack saw as he looked into house after house, all slept peacefully, untroubled by nightmares. They were happy. Everyone here was happy!

Jack could not keep from smiling. He was happy, too! Amazing! What is this? he wondered. And then he saw the sign:

CHRISTMASTOWN

'Christmastown?' Jack murmured to himself. 'Hmmm . . .'

Back in Hollowe'enland, nobody was smiling. Far from it. There were frowns, there were groans, and there were moans, because Jack was still missing. This fact was causing everyone a great deal of worry.

'We've got to find Jack!' the Mayor told the crowd that had gathered in the town square. 'There are only three hundred and sixty-five days left till next Hallowe'en!'

'Three hundred and sixty-four!' yelled an especially worried werewolf.

'Is there anywhere we've forgotten to

check?' asked the Mayor. 'Think hard. Tell me.'

'I looked in the crypts,' said a vampire.

'We opened the tombs,' called the witches.

'I scoured the cemetery,' said the werewolf. 'But he wasn't there.'

Worries deepened. Moods darkened. Where *was* he?

'It's time to sound the alarm,' said the Mayor.

The wail of a cat screeching was the town's alarm. The distant noise reached Sally's ears just as she was whipping up a very special brew. Her private name for it was Sleeping Potion Soup, though when she served it up to the Evil Scientist she simply called it lunch. It was full of deadly nightshade, and if the doctor drank it, he'd sleep for a week.

Wouldn't *that* be nice, thought Sally as she set a steaming bowl of the stuff in front of the doctor. Then I could get away. For good.

'Have some,' she urged. The doctor sniffed it hungrily, but then put down his spoon. 'Frog's breath!' he snarled.

'What's wrong?' said Sally innocently. 'I thought you liked frog's breath.' But inwardly she quailed. She had used frog's breath to disguise the smell of deadly nightshade. Had she used too much?

'Nothing's more suspicious than frog's breath,' said the doctor. He dipped his spoon into the soup and held it up to Sally. 'Until *you* taste it,' he told he, '*I* won't swallow a spoonful.'

Sally knocked the spoon out of his hand with a nervous giggle. 'I'm not hungry,' she said.

The doctor fixed her with his most malevolent glare. 'You want me to starve, don't you? I'm weak. I'm old. And you owe your very life to me!'

'Oh, don't be silly,' said Sally. She bent down as if to pick up the spoon, then reached into her sock and pulled out a slotted spoon instead. She dipped into the soup and noisily pretended to slurp up a mouthful of broth.

It worked! Thanks to the slotted spoon, the soup fell back into the bowl, but the doctor didn't see. Sally breathed a huge sigh of relief as he grabbed the bowl away from her and started eating hungrily.

'See?' she said as he gobbled it down. 'It's scrumptious.' A hopeful smile crept over her rag-doll face. Soon, she thought. Soon I'll be free.

CHAPTER FOUR

Back in the town square, hope was as scarce as bat feathers. Despair, however, was readily available. The Mayor, who lay sprawled on top of his hearse, had more than enough for everyone. As dusk fell he stared up at the darkening sky in desperation. Where was Jack?

No one knew.

Then, just as a sliver of moon appeared in the sky, a distant bark was heard. It was followed by a strange rumbling sound, a sound that gradually grew louder and louder.

'Zero . . .? Jack . . .?' The Mayor barely

dared to say the words aloud. He sat up. The crowd stirred.

The rumbling became a dull roar. Jack, driving a jaunty red Christmastown snowmobile, zoomed into the square. Zero followed, his nose all aglow, barking with excitement.

A ragged cheer went up in the square. The Mayor, wavering between relief and irritation, naturally chose irritation. 'Where have you been?' he snapped. 'We've been worried sick!'

'Call a town meeting and I'll tell you all about it!' answered Jack with a smile.

Jack was still smiling as the town hall filled up a few hours later. He had great news to tell, and everyone seemed a bit confused, but eager to hear about it. Sally, fresh from putting the Evil Scientist to sleep, pressed forward with the rest of the crowd. As Jack stepped up to the podium, a murmur of interest and excitement swept through the hall. But when Jack tried to describe Christmastown, the interest turned to puzzlement.

Christmastown? What was that?

'It's a world unlike any I've ever seen,' said Jack. 'I . . . I can't describe it, but it's not a dream – it's as real as my skull!' The crowd looked bewildered. Luckily Jack had come prepared. He turned to the table beside him, which was piled high with Christmas presents.

'Here, let me show you,' he said, holding up a gaily wrapped box. 'This is called a present. The whole thing starts with a box –'

'A pox?' asked a demon. 'How delightful, a pox!'

'No!' cried Jack, whose smile was beginning to fade. 'A *box*, with brightly coloured paper and a bow!'

'A bow?' said a witch. 'But why?'

'How very ugly!' said another witch.

'What's in it, anyway?'

'The point of the thing is not to know,' said Jack.

Not to know? What was Jack talking about? Confusion swept through the crowd like wind over a bog. Jack decided to try something else. He held up a big red Christmas stocking.

'In Christmastown,' he said, 'an oversized sock like this is hung on the wall –'

'Does it still have a foot in it?' someone interrupted. 'Let me look!'

'Let *me* see!' called someone else. 'Is it rotted and covered with gook?'

By now there was not a trace of a smile on Jack's face, and his frustration was beginning to show. 'There's no foot inside,' he told the crowd as patiently as he could. 'There're sweets, or sometimes it's filled with small toys.'

'Small toys?'

'Do they bite?'

'Do they snap?'

'Do they scare girls and boys?'

Jack saw that he was getting nowhere fast. This crowd could never understand the goodwill and good cheer of Christmas. I may as well give them what they want, he decided. Scary, spooky Hallowe'enland-type stuff. He leaned forward as if he were confiding a dark secret.

'I've saved the best for last,' he said. 'The ruler of Christmastown is a fearsome king with a deep, mighty voice. And on the darkest of nights, he flies into the air – "slaying" through the sky!'

Hearing this, the crowd grew very quiet.

'He is huge and red, like a giant lobster,' Jack continued. 'They call him . . . Sandy Claws!' His words sent a thrill through the audience. As they broke into excited chatter Jack slowly gathered up his Christmastown souvenirs. The meeting hadn't exactly turned out the way he'd hoped. Everyone was excited, but no one really understood why Christmastown was so special. Could he ever make them see? Jack sighed and headed for home. He just didn't know.

CHAPTER FIVE

But after spending the night in his tower, surrounded by all his Christmastown paraphernalia – the snow globes, the liquorice sticks, the holly – Jack was determined to try again. This time he would do it differently. Methodically. Scientifically. He snapped his bony fingers.

'That's it!' he cried. 'I'll conduct a series of experiments and isolate the Christmas spirit – scientifically! Stroke of genius, Jack!'

After a quick trip to the now-recovered Evil Scientist's house to borrow equipment,

Jack got to work. First he set up a laboratory at the top of his tower, complete with microscope, centrifuge, test tubes, Petri dishes and beakers. Then he began testing various objects for the Christmas spirit. He began with mistletoe. No luck. Then he tried a liquorice stick and a teddy bear. Still no luck. His eye fell on a group of bright Christmas decorations: globes, angels and a glittering star.

'Hmmm,' he murmured. 'It's worth a try.' He crushed the star and poured the dust into a beaker. At first nothing happened. Then it began to glow and pulsate, filling the room with a beautiful soft green light. What was it? What did it mean? Jack didn't know.

Not far away, someone else was watching that pulsing green light. As Jack stood in his tower room transfixed by its unearthly glow, Sally the Rag Doll saw it from the window, high up in her room, where the Evil Scientist had locked her.

Sally wanted to escape from the doctor more than ever. But for the first time in her lonely rag-doll life, she yearned to escape *to* someone. And that someone was Jack. Sally had fallen in love with him.

She had decided to send him a gift – a special potion she had prepared for herself. She put the potion into a basket and lowered it out of her window on a rope. The ground was so far away! For an instant Sally lost her courage. But the thought of Jack brought it back to her. The basket landed on the ground, and Sally gathered up all her resolve. Then she jumped.

The thud she made was soft enough that no one, least of all the Evil Scientist, heard it. So even though she had lost an arm and a leg in the fall, Sally didn't mind. She was clever. She had come prepared. She pulled out her trusty darning needle and proceeded to sew herself back together again. It didn't take long. Moments later she was standing at the foot of Jack's tower, fastening her basket to the rope and pulley that hung from Jack's window.

When Sally's basket arrived, Jack was in the middle of yet another equation. This one read: Presents + Mistletoe + Snowballs = Christmas Fun. It looked as good as all the others. Why weren't any of them adding up right? Jack scratched his skull. It was aching.

The basket at his window was a welcome interruption. So was Sally, who stood far below, beaming up at him. The sight cheered Jack immensely, though he couldn't say why. Then he noticed a bottle in the basket. He opened it. A tiny cloud drifted out of the bottle and took shape in the air above Jack's head. It became a ghostly butterfly, beautiful and haunting.

How lovely! thought Jack. He leaned out

of the window to thank Sally, but she had disappeared.

Though she was extremely clever and brave enough to jump seventeen metres to the ground, Sally was also a little shy. The moment Jack had smiled down at her, she had been seized by a fit of shyness so overpowering that it had whisked her away from his tower like a turbo-charged witch's broom. Now she sat at the town gates, wondering what the future held. Well, there was one way to find out.

Sally picked a flower and began pulling off its petals one by one. 'He loves me, he loves me not,' she whispered. 'He loves me. He –' Suddenly the flower in Sally's hand did something very strange. It began to twirl around, then changed into a miniature Christmas tree!

Sally stared at it, not knowing what to think. Did this mean that Jack didn't love her? Or was it a bad omen about his plans for Christmas? She just didn't know. Suddenly the tiny tree burst into flames and disappeared, leaving Sally cold, confused and completely in the dark.

Jack Skellington, the head haunt of Hallowe'enland, has grown tired of the same old frights.

Sally the Rag Doll hides behind a tombstone, listening to Jack's song of woe.

Zero, Jack's trusty ghost dog, accompanies his master wherever he roams.

While wandering through the forest, Jack comes upon a tree with a mysterious door carved into its trunk.

On the other side of the door, Jack finds Christmastown, a strange but wonderful new place.

Jack calls a meeting of all Hallowe'enland's ghouls and ghosts to tell them about the wonders of Christmastown.

Jack tries to get into the Christmas spirit by making a snowflake, but doesn't get it quite right.

Not knowing any better, Jack takes a scientific approach to understanding Christmas.

Lock, Shock, and Barrel, Hallowe'enland's most devious trick-or-treaters, head off to kidnap Santa Claus.

Kidnapped by mistake, the Easter Bunny meets one of Hallowe'enland's citizens.

'Trick or treat!' – Lock, Shock, and Barrel finally find 'Sandy Claws'.

Santa is surprised to find trick-or-treaters on his doorstep on Christmas Eve.

With Santa out of the way, Jack begins delivering his own brand of Christmas Cheer.

Despite Jack's good intentions, his presents end up frightening everyone.

In Hallowe'enland there really is a boogie man, and his name is Oogie Boogie.

Standing together on a snow-covered hill, Sally and Jack look forward to next year's Hallowe'en.

CHAPTER SIX

Sally wasn't the only one who was in the dark that night. Up in his tower, Jack was completely befuddled also. He'd done fifty-six more equations. He'd experimented with everything from toy trains to tinsel. He'd read Christmas stories and memorized Christmas carols. He'd been methodical. He'd been scientific. He'd been . . . unsuccessful. For in spite of all his calculations, Jack still hadn't been able to isolate the Christmas spirit. He felt as far from a solution now as when he'd started.

He groaned, covering his eyes in despair.

When he opened them, they fell on the beaker, glowing green, on his table. Its light was softer now, but still beautiful. As he looked at it, Jack felt better. He would find his answer, no matter how long it took.

And then, like a bolt of lightning, it came to him. I've been doing this all wrong! he realized. I can never turn Hallowe'enland into Christmastown. It's impossible. We're too different. But that's all right. We can have something even better. *We* can make presents for all the boys and girls of the world. We can have Christmas *our* way.

Jack grinned. It was time for another town meeting.

The Mayor was confused. One minute there was one town meeting. The next minute there was *another* town meeting. All these meetings were making him dizzy! What was going on?

But for all his confusion, the Mayor knew

that a good leader should be decisive, or at least look that way. So he was careful to put on his very best smiling, in-charge face once he joined Jack inside the town hall. Maybe this crazy idea of making a Hallowe'enland Christmas would work. The important thing was to act as if it were all perfectly normal, all part of a master plan that he, the Mayor, had helped to engineer.

But oh, it was hard. The Mayor did his best to look as if he knew what was happening while Jack gave out assignments. The werewolves were to make Christmas biscuits, the Evil Scientist was to make those strange flying animals with the branches on their heads, and the vampires were to make baby dolls. Jack was getting everyone in Hallowe'enland involved, including Lock, Shock and Barrel, Hallowe'enland's professional trick-or-treaters.

When they showed up, smiling mischievously, wearing those silly masks of theirs, the Mayor shivered. It wasn't that the little devil, witch and ghoul were trick-or-treaters. That was a fine profession in Hallowe'enland. No, it was something else.

Lock, Shock and Barrel were scheming. They were clever. And they always had something up their sleeves. Worse, the creature they called their leader, the one who had shaped them into their troublemaking little selves, was Oogie Boogie. When he thought of Oogie, the Mayor couldn't help it. He screamed.

Mean, fiendish Oogie was a giant, bulging sack, stuffed with nasty insects and snakes that had a way of crawling through his badly stitched seams. His favourite activity was prowling through the dark, looking for things – or people – to eat. Oogie was always hungry. He was the scariest creature in Hallowe'enland.

'Jack! Jack!' the Mayor yelped. 'It's Oogie's boys!'

Jack simply smiled. Amazing! He actually looked glad to see those little demons. 'Ah, Hallowe'en's finest trick-or-treaters,' he said, leaning down to pat each of them on the head. 'The job I have for you is top secret. It requires craft and cunning.'

Shock's eyes twinkled behind her witch's mask. 'And we thought you didn't like us, Jack,' she said with a cackle.

Jack knelt down so he could whisper. 'Absolutely no one is to know about it. Not a soul!'

The Mayor couldn't believe it. Not only had Jack actually invited Lock, Shock and Barrel here, now he was cooking up some kind of secret plan with them! What was going on?

Jack hardly noticed the Mayor's curiosity. He was busy telling Lock, Shock and Barrel the most important part of his plan, the part about Sandy Claws. When he finished he looked at them long and hard. 'One more thing,' he said. 'Leave Oogie Boogie out of this.'

'Of course, Jack,' said Lock.

'Whatever you say, Jack,' said Shock.

'We wouldn't dream of it, Jack,' said Barrel.

And one by one they crossed their fingers behind their backs. They were lying! But how could Jack know that?

As the three little monsters hurried out of the town hall, giggling merrily, Jack smiled after them. His dream, he thought, was coming true. Little did he know that it was rapidly turning into a nightmare.

Lock, Shock and Barrel loved nightmares. Gleefully they hurried home to their tree house, which was perched on a gnarled old tree on top of a steep ravine. Once there, the terrible threesome sat down and took off their masks. They smiled at each other. Their real faces were exactly the same as their masks, but no one in Hallowe'enland knew that except Oogie Boogie.

They began to plan their crime. How to do it?

Lock, who often thought out loud for the group, said they should set a trap for Sandy Claws, then throw him in a big lobster pot where he belonged. Then Lock had a better idea. What if they went to his door with a cannon? That might be fun.

Shock, the brains of the operation, was scornful. What good would Sandy Claws be blown to bits and pieces? Jack wouldn't like that. Then again, how important was Jack's opinion? After they kidnapped Sandy – in one piece, of course – they could bring him to Jack for a moment, but then he should go to Oogie Boogie. After all, they worked for Oogie. They had to stay on his good side. And what could

39

please him more than a big, fat, juicy lobster-man? The trio giggled in agreement. Great idea! They climbed into their claw-footed bath and zoomed off in search of their prey.

CHAPTER SEVEN

Of course, Jack knew nothing of Lock, Shock and Barrel's plans. He was too busy working on his own plans, which were becoming more elaborate by the minute. He was handing out assignments to everyone in Hallowe'enland, from the smallest gremlin to the biggest behemoth. If he had his way, everyone would take part in Christmas, even Hallowe'enland's own band that played mournful tunes out on the street every day. Surely, if they tried, they could learn to play 'Jingle Bells'?

When Jack asked them, they assured

him that they could. Like most folks in Hallowe'enland, they found it hard to say no to Jack. They liked him and would follow where he led, even into unfamiliar territory.

Sally, of course, not only liked Jack, she loved him. So when he came to her at the meeting and said, 'Sally, I need your help more than anyone's,' how could she say no?

He wanted her to sew him a Sandy Claws outfit, and she would do it. But Sally's heart wasn't in it. In fact, her heart was full of dread about Jack's plans. She kept thinking about the strange omen she'd had, of the Christmas tree going up in flames. It frightened her. But when she tried to tell Jack about it, she didn't get very far.

'Jack,' she said. 'Please listen to me. It's going to be a disaster.'

'How could it be?' he replied, showing her a drawing of a Sandy Claws suit. 'Just follow the pattern!'

Sally tried again. 'It's a mistake, Jack,' she said, seeing once again in her mind that terrible burning tree.

But it was no use. The only thing Jack wanted to think about was his suit.

'Don't be so modest,' Jack told her. 'No one else but you is clever enough to sew this for me!'

Finally Sally gave up. If she couldn't save Jack, thought Sally, she might as well sew for him. She headed for the town square, where Christmas preparations were in full swing.

Just as Sally left the town hall, Lock, Shock and Barrel raced in. They were dragging a big sack with something squirming inside of it.

'Jack!' they shouted. 'We caught him! We've got him!'

Jack's heart pounded. 'Open it up! Hurry!' he cried.

Giggling with excitement, the trick-or-treaters opened their sack. Out jumped an enormous pink rabbit. It did not look happy.

'That's not Sandy Claws!' said Jack.

'It isn't?' asked Shock.

'Who is it?' said Barrel.

Jack didn't know. He had never seen a rabbit before, much less a giant Easter Bunny like this. But he was sure of one thing. This wasn't Sandy Claws!

When he said so, Lock, Shock and Barrel protested.

'We followed your instructions,' whined Lock.

'We went through the door,' said Barrel.

'Which door?' asked Jack. 'I told you there'd be more than one. You were supposed to go through the tree-shaped door!' He held up a cut-out of a Christmas tree.

'Take him back!' he ordered.

The trick-or-treaters were disappointed. So they did what all nasty little demons do when they're disappointed. They started to blame each other. It soon erupted into a huge fight. Shock grabbed Lock's throat. Barrel pounded Shock on the head.

Jack, normally a patient fellow, found his patience with the trio running out. So he did something he usually saved for the darkest hour of Hallowe'en night. He rattled his bones at them. It was a fearsome sound, and it worked. The trio stopped fighting.

In the silence, Jack turned to the Easter Bunny, whose pink nose was twitching in terror. 'I'm terribly sorry for the inconvenience, sir,' he said. 'If you'll kindly step back into this sack, my friends will escort you home.'

The Easter Bunny didn't need another word of encouragement. He bounded straight back into the sack. As Lock, Shock and Barrel carried him away, Jack shouted after them, 'Take him home first! Apologize again! And be careful with

Sandy Claws when you fetch him! Treat him nicely!'

Jack watched the three trick-or-treaters leave and took a deep breath. Being a mastermind was not easy.

But it did have its rewards, as he discovered the next day. The moment he saw the Hallowe'eners preparing Christmas in the town square, Jack's heart began to sing. Everything he saw, from the Evil Scientist working hard on his skeleton reindeer to Sally stitching away on a magnificent red Sandy Claws suit, was like a wonderful dream come true. He skipped through the town square, so happy that his bony feet barely touched the floor.

There was so much to admire! At one table, a team of vampires strung tiny skull-shaped lights; at another, a group of witches made baby voodoo dolls; and at a third, Hallowe'enland's hardest-working werewolves toiled away at a magnificent goblin-in-the-box. Jack fairly hummed with joy. This was going to be the most amazing Christmas ever!

Santa Claus thought so, too. Far off in Christmastown, while his elves assembled beautiful toys and baked mouth-watering biscuits, cakes and pies, Santa sat in his snow-covered cottage, making his list and checking it twice.

What he read made him shake his head in astonishment. 'Nice . . . nice . . . naughty . . . nice . . . nice . . . nice. Amazing!' he murmured. 'There are hardly any naughty children this year.' His ruddy face beamed. This is going to be a Christmas to remember, he thought happily.

At that moment his doorbell rang. 'Now who could that be?' mused Santa. Reluctantly setting his list down, he lifted himself out of his armchair and walked to the door.

When he opened it, he saw three strange little children smiling up at him. Why were they dressed like a witch, a devil and a ghoul? Why were they carrying that huge sack? And what, Santa wondered, before everything suddenly went black, did they mean by 'trick or treat'?

CHAPTER EIGHT

'You don't look like yourself, Jack, not at all,' said Sally the Rag Doll. She and Jack were in the town square, and she was helping him on with his new red coat. Sally didn't like much about this strange Christmas holiday, and she didn't like the red coat, either, even though she had sewn it herself. Jack looked so much better, she thought, in the elegant black suit he usually wore.

But Jack was ecstatic. 'Isn't this wonderful? It couldn't be more wonderful!' he exclaimed as he buttoned up the coat.

'But you're the Pumpkin King,' said Sally, wishing Jack would come to his senses.

He didn't even hear her. As far as he was concerned, he was a million miles from Hallowe'en. Tonight was Christmas Eve, and he was ready for it!

His wonderful coffin-shaped sleigh was loaded with gifts made by the Hallowe'en people. He was wearing a magnificent Sandy Claws costume, and soon – any minute now! – he would be taking off on the adventure of his dreams.

Jack looked at himself in a mirror. Something, he realized, was missing. What was it? He had the coat, the boots, even the big white beard.

Just then he heard his name being called – by Lock, Shock and Barrel.

'Jack! Jack! We bagged him!' they shrieked, scuttling into the square. They were dragging a huge sack.

'This time we really did it!' crowed Barrel. 'He sure is big!'

'And heavy!' added Shock, panting.

'Let me out!' rumbled a voice from inside. Suddenly the sack heaved, rolled and opened. Out stepped a big fat man with white hair and a white beard. His red clothes were rumpled, his red stocking cap was askew, and his very red face was wet with sweat.

Jack was thrilled. 'Sandy Claws!' he cried. 'In person! What a pleasure to meet you!'

Santa Claus was not a young man, but he had lived a sheltered life. He had spent most of it with jolly, hardworking elves and the rest with sleeping children, who were at their most angelic because they weren't awake. Making beautiful, festive Christmas gifts and then delivering them to good little girls and boys had not prepared him for – this.

He looked around in horror. Ghouls and monsters, one uglier than the next, pressed in on him, their faces twitching with curiosity. Who were they? And this tall, bony fellow, who was obviously their leader, kept beaming at him foolishly. Why? Santa's mind whirled with a dozen unspoken questions.

'Surprised, aren't you?' said the bony fellow. 'I knew you would be! You don't need to have a single worry about Christmas this year. We're handling it. You can have the night off.'

Santa's heart nearly stopped. What was this skeleton talking about? Christmas Eve was the high point of his entire year! He had reindeer to drive! Gifts to deliver! And now he was going to be late!

'But, I – !' he gasped, nearly speechless with dismay.

'Think of this as a holiday, Sandy,' the bony fellow said. 'A chance for you to relax and take it easy.' Then he realized what his Sandy Claws costume was missing. He plucked the red cap from Santa's head. 'While you rest,' he said, 'I'll just borrow this.'

Worry, anger and fear did not help Santa's powers of speech. Before he could manage a reply, the terrible trio who had kidnapped him were dragging him away. Wouldn't anybody help him? This was a nightmare!

'No . . . please . . . wait . . .!' he begged. But the trick-or-treaters' giggling drowned out his pleas.

This is a nightmare! thought Sally the Rag Doll as poor Santa was hauled off. All her fears about Christmas were turning out to be true. It was a disaster. She had to do something. She racked her rag-doll brain. 'I know!' she whispered, and slipped away.

Jack, entranced with Santa's red cap, never saw her leave. The cap, he thought, was just the thing to complete his dazzling Christmas outfit. He adjusted it so it sat at a rakish angle on his skull, then got ready to climb into his sleigh. Once the Mayor finished his farewell speech, Jack could be off.

Jack looked up towards the Mayor and blinked. He and everyone else in the crowd looked around in disbelief. A thick white fog had appeared out of nowhere and was swirling through the town square. It was soupy. It was sinister. It was as bone-chilling and blinding as the fog that came on Hallowe'en. And like that fog, it had swallowed everything up.

'Oh no!' groaned Jack. 'We'll never be able to take off in this. The reindeer can't see an inch in front of their noses.'

Out of the fog came moans and complaints, a loud monster chorus of disappointment. Christmas was ruined! How could this be?

Safely hidden by clouds of white mist, one face smiled in relief: the face of Sally the Rag Doll. For it was Sally, of course, who had mixed up a special potion and dumped it in the town fountain. The fog was her creation. Deep in her rag-doll stuffing Sally felt that Christmas could not go on, and she had to stop it. Now it looked as if she had succeeded.

She peered through the thick fog at Jack. Had he given up?

No! He was talking to Zero, his little ghost dog, who hovered in the air with his jack-o'-lantern nose glowing. 'Zero, with your nose so bright,' Jack asked, 'won't you guide my sleigh tonight?' Zero's answer was a bark of excitement and a loop-the-loop through the air.

'I guess that means yes,' said Jack with a grin. He turned to the crowd. 'My friends,' he announced happily, 'Christmas is saved! Zero is going to lead my sleigh through the fog!'

As the crowd whistled and cheered, Zero took his place at the head of the reindeer, his nose shining like a beacon. Jack leapt aboard and cracked his whip.

'We're off!' he cried. 'Ho! Ho! Ho!' The sleigh rose into the air to wild applause. Only one note of worry sounded in the crowd, and it was so soft and so sad that not a single creature heard it.

'Good-bye, Jack,' whispered Sally. 'Oh, how I hope my premonition is wrong!'

As Sally wandered away from the town square, her heart heavy with dread, and as Jack sailed through the skies laughing with joy, Lock, Shock and Barrel were having a brief, but very interesting, discussion about their prisoner, Santa Claus.

'So, where are we taking him?' asked Barrel.

'To Oogie Boogie, of course,' said Lock and Shock.

'Of course!' said Barrel with a nervous giggle. 'Oogie will like that.'

Santa didn't know who Oogie Boogie

was. But he did know that Christmas was in grave danger. Why wouldn't these three let him go?

'Haven't you ever heard of peace on earth and goodwill to men?' he asked from inside the sack, struggling to get free.

'No!' cried the trio gleefully. They tightened their grip. This was so much fun!

Jack was having fun as well. He was spreading Christmas cheer throughout the world. Or so he thought. On his first stop, the little boy in the house where he crash-landed had stared at him in silence when he came slithering down the chimney. But when Jack handed the boy a present – one of his very own special shrunken heads – the cries of joy from the little fellow were very loud. Very loud, indeed.

Jack had no idea that he had just given an innocent child the most bloodcurdling shock of his young life. And those sounds he heard as he drove off in his sleigh? They were far from cries of joy. They were shrieks of horror.

As Jack continued on his rounds, delivering dozens of creepy, dark and gloomy Christmas presents, he heard many shrieks. There were shrieks for the wreath with long arms. Shrieks for the toy gravedigger's kit. Shrieks for the miniature electric chair. There were bloodcurdling screams for the eyeball marbles and the slug farms.

Jack was pleased to hear them. But, of course, he didn't know any better. When people screamed, 'These presents are horrible!' he thought he was hearing shouts of delight.

So one and on he went, merrily delivering his dreadful gifts, unaware of the havoc he was creating. Time after time he mistook shouts of anger and disgust for cries of gratitude and answered them with a cheerful

'Merry Christmas!' He never heard the doors slamming, the locks clicking, or the frantic telephone calls to the police. As far as Jack was concerned, everyone was having a wonderful time.

He didn't know it, but down below, Jack was considered a criminal. And like a criminal, he was being hunted down – with very powerful guns.

But when Jack first saw the bright searchlights and heard the explosions of gunfire he was actually pleased.

'Look, Zero!' he cried. 'They're celebrating! They're thanking us for doing such a good job!'

Then gunfire nearly struck one of the reindeer. And it began to dawn on Jack that something was very, very wrong . . .

CHAPTER TEN

Long before Jack began to worry, Sally the Rag Doll *knew* that something was wrong. She had seen the explosions in the sky, and the witchvine was abuzz with grim reports that Jack's trip was in trouble.

Something told Sally that if anyone could help, it was Santa. But where was he? At best, he'd be with Lock, Shock and Barrel. At worst . . . he'd be with Oogie Boogie. Sally shuddered from head to toe. What a frightening thought!

But something told her it was so. Sally knew what Lock, Shock and Barrel were like. And she knew there was only one place those nasty little trick-or-treaters would take their captive – to the underground torture chamber that evil Oogie called home.

So Sally headed for Oogie's lair. And there a terrible sight met her eyes. Oogie's dungeon was dark and dank, wreathed in cobwebs, littered with bones. It was a miserable, hopeless place, and right smack at its centre lay Santa, bound hand and foot. On a giant roulette table was arranged a strange array of gambling paraphernalia – from worm-ridden dice to slot machines designed to shoot real bullets. Standing over Santa, grinning with malice, was Oogie Boogie. His huge, bag-like body was filled with buzzing bugs, which crawled in and out of his gaping mouth.

Oogie was doing his best to make Santa miserable, and he was succeeding. But then, being creepy, scary and disgusting was Oogie's job. He was the boogie man, after all. As Sally watched in horror, Oogie danced around Santa, threatening him.

'You're ugly, old man, but you might be tasty,' he said, rolling his dice. 'And I'm getting hungry. Want to be the main ingredient in a nice snake-and-spider stew? I'll boil you alive! How about it?'

'No!' cried Santa. 'Let me go! Please! The children are expecting me. I've got to deliver their Christmas presents!'

'Ha, ha, ha!' Oogie replied. 'It's hopeless. You're finished! You haven't got a prayer. 'Cause I'm the big bad boogie man, and you ain't goin' nowhere!'

Santa writhed and strained at the ropes that bound him, but it was no use. He couldn't get free. Oogie loomed closer . . . and closer . . . and closer . . .

Meanwhile, high in the sky, a missile was moving closer and closer and closer to Jack. When it hit, it destroyed the sleigh instantly and sent Jack on a dizzying, all-too-rapid fall to earth.

Jack landed in the arms of a stone angel in a cemetery. His jaw-bone had come unhinged in the fall, so for a moment he lay there silently. He was unable to speak and unable to avoid the terrible truth: his version of Christmas was a complete and total failure. This thought was far more painful than the shock of falling.

What a fool he had been! What a stupid mistake he had made! If Jack's jaw had been attached, he would have groaned in frustration. But it wasn't. So he simply lay there and waited for Zero to retrieve his lost part.

'Good dog,' he murmured as soon as Zero brought it to him. Slowly Jack put himself together. And as he did, he made up his mind.

He would set things right! But to do that, he had to find Sandy Claws – fast. Could he do it?

'I've got to try, Zero,' he told his faithful dog. 'I just hope there's still time.'

Filled with resolve, he dashed to a tombstone, lifted it and hurried down a long flight of steps to Hallowe'enland.

CHAPTER ELEVEN

Lock, Shock and Barrel were having fun. As usual, it was because someone else wasn't.

Perched above the trapdoor to Oogie Boogie's dungeon, they looked on as Oogie tormented not one prisoner but two! Sally the Rag Doll's desperate attempt to rescue Santa had backfired, and now she was Oogie's captive, too.

But just as the three trick-or-treaters leaned in to get a better look, they heard a dreadful sound behind them. A sound like the rattle of skeleton bones. Could it be? It was! Jack Skellington. Shrieking in terror, the three of them turned and ran off into the night.

Jack took their place at the trapdoor. Far below he could see Santa and Sally strapped to a table over a steaming cauldron. In spite of her plight, the brave rag doll was still defiant. 'This isn't over!' she cried. 'Not by a long shot! You wait till Jack hears about this. By the time he's through with you, you'll be lucky if –'

At that moment the Mayor's voice interrupted her. It came blaring over a loudspeaker from his hearse out in the street, and the news it delivered was terrible.

'The king of Hallowe'en has been blown to smithereens,' announced the Mayor. 'Jack Skellington is now a pile of dust.'

Sally heard this, and tears came to her eyes. Oogie heard it and roared with triumph. If Jack was gone, *he* would be king of Hallowe'enland!

'A pile of dust!' he repeated gleefully, turning to his captives. He smiled hungrily. 'And dust *to* dust.' Dancing a little victory dance, he sang, 'Ooh, I'm feeling hungry. One more roll of the dice ought to do it!'

He tossed his giant dice. They rolled across the dungeon floor, finally coming to a stop with two ones showing. 'What! Snake eyes?' Oogie roared, and pounded the floor with his fist until the dice bounced back, this time showing eleven.

Oogie grinned in satisfaction. 'Looks like I won the jackpot!' Turning the crank of the torture machine, he began to lower Sally and Santa into the enormous steaming cauldron. 'Bye-bye, Dollface and Sandman!' he bellowed as they screamed. Giving the crank one last turn, he dropped the table below the cauldron's rim.

The boogie man cackled as he waited to hear his victims' final splash. But there was nothing. No sound at all.

'Huh?' he said. Reversing the crank, he slowly drew the board back up from the cauldron. There, instead of Sandy Claws and Sally the Rag Doll, was Jack Skellington!

'Hello, Oogie,' said Jack, leaping nimbly from the table and on to the roulette wheel.

'Jack?' cried Oogie, drawing back in fright. 'But they said you were dead! You must be *double dead*!'

Stomping on a lever near his foot, Oogie sent the roulette wheel spinning, throwing Jack off balance. Immediately a ring of giant playing cards, each showing the king of spades, rose up around the edges of the wheel. The kings, coming to life, lunged at Jack with very real swords. Dodging wildly, Jack managed to stay just out of reach of their twirling weapons. He was so distracted he didn't notice an enormous billiard ball descending from the ceiling, its sides splitting open into spinning blades.

Oogie laughed maniacally as Jack weaved around the wheel, trying desperately to dodge both dangers. The bugs in Oogie's sack-like body flew this way and that, making his sides heave and bulge. 'Well, come on, Bone Man!' he said, pulling a chain above his head. The cards' flailing swords folded in and the cards retracted, but instantly an army of one-armed slot machines rolled forward.

'Fire!' shouted Oogie, and the machines began shooting from their loaded arms. Quick as a wink, Jack leapt on top of one of them. Cursing in frustration, the boogie man reached for another button and sent the roulette wheel flying towards Jack.

'Look out!' screeched Sally. Just in time Jack jumped out of the way, letting the wheel's revolving blade slice off the arms of each of the shooting slot machines. The rag doll sighed with relief. Jack jumped again, landing in front of Oogie. Now they could have a fair fight. But just then the boogie man stepped on to another lever.

'So long!' he shouted, catapulting himself up to the top of the billiard ball and out of Jack's reach.

Jack looked up at him. 'How dare you treat my friends so shamefully,' he said in a quiet voice. Reaching up with a bony arm, he tugged on a small string hanging low from Boogie's body.

For Sally and Santa, watching from the corner of the dungeon, it took a moment to realize what was happening. Slowly at first, but then more and more rapidly, the boogie man began to unravel. Though Oogie wriggled and writhed, there was nothing he could do. In a matter of seconds there was only a mass of loose bugs where he had been.

'Now look what you've done,' Oogie's voice cried pitifully from the swarm of creeping insects. 'My bugs, my bugs!'

Creeping, crawling and flying, all the insects except one quickly dispersed. Then, *splat!* Santa squashed the last bug with his big black boot.

Oogie Boogie was gone for good.

Sally beamed with relief. Santa wiped his damp forehead. And Jack apologized.

'Forgive me, Sandy Claws,' he said. 'I'm afraid I've made a *terrible* mess of your holiday.'

'Bumpy sleigh ride, Jack?' said Santa. 'Christmas is a lot more than a bag of toys and a red cap!' Snatching his hat from Jack's head, he turned to leave.

'I hope there's still time,' Jack called after him.

'Of course there is,' said the old elf. 'I'm Santa Claus.' And with that, he pressed a finger to the side of his nose and shot up the narrow tube that led outside.

'He'll fix things, Jack. He knows what to do,' said Sally, trying to make him feel better.

Jack turned to the rag doll. Suddenly it was as though he was seeing her for the very first time. 'How did you get down here?' he asked.

'I was trying to . . . well, I wanted to . . .' The little doll blushed and fell silent.

'To help me?' asked Jack. 'Why, Sally, I never realized . . .'

Just then a booming voice rang out. 'Jack! Jack!' The Mayor appeared with Lock, Shock and Barrel following right behind him.

'Here he is!' said Shock.

'Alive!' said Lock.

'Just like we said,' Barrel chimed in.

'Grab ahold, my boy!' cried the Mayor, lowering a ladder into the late Oogie's lair. 'Everyone's waiting from you!' He and the trick-or-treaters pulled Jack out of the dungeon and into the town square.

As Jack appeared, the adoring crowd cheered its greeting.

And then another greeting was heard – from the sky. 'Ho! Ho! Ho!' came a deep, jolly voice from above. 'Merry Christmas to one and all!'

The citizens of Hallowe'enland looked up. There was Santa Claus, sailing across the moon in a sleigh laden with gifts. Jack waved at him. As if in reply, something soft, white and cool drifted down. It was Santa's Christmas gift to Hallowe'enland – snow!

A cry of goodwill and happiness filled the air. The Christmas spirit had come to Hallowe'enland at last.

High above the town square, Sally the Rag Doll watched the celebration with a wistful smile on her face. The moon was full. The snow was beautiful. The world was content. Only Sally's heart was filled with yearning.

She sighed. Would her loneliness ever end? Would Jack ever love her, too? She picked a flower and pulled off its petals one by one. 'He loves me, he loves me not,' she whispered.

A long, elegant figure made its way across the snowy ground until it stood next to her. Sally the Rag Doll looked up, hardly daring to hope.

'He loves you,' said Jack Skellington.

E P I L O G U E

Santa never forgot that Christmas Eve; it was the longest one of his life. But though it was frightening, even terrifying at times, Santa remembers Jack Skellington fondly.

For the truth is that Santa actually enjoyed himself that night. In a strange way, one he hardly understands, the thrills and chills were actually fun. Of course, Santa has never revealed this to another living soul – not even to Mrs Claus or his most trusted elves.

They never suspect that every now and then, when he's feeling just the tiniest bit bored with his jolly, cheer-delivering life, Santa climbs into his sleigh and disappears for a while.

And where does he go?

To Hallowe'enland, to visit Jack.

And there the two old friends sit, reminiscing about the way they met and sharing a joke or two about Jack's fascination with Christmas – and Santa's secret affection for Hallowe'en.

At the end of every visit, Santa always asks Jack the same question.

'Jack, my boy,' he says with a twinkle in his eye, 'if you had it to do all over again, would you? Could you?'

To which Jack always replies, with a smile of pure delight, 'Of course I would. Wouldn't you?'

FREE WILLY

A novelisation by Todd Strasser

Willy is a mighty killer whale. Jesse is an eleven-year-old runaway who never had a real home. Together they form a very special friendship.

The star attraction at an amusement park, Willy is restless and longs to be reunited with his family at sea. The park owner, however, has decided that the whale is worth more dead than alive. Can Jesse free Willy before its too late?

FRANKENSTEIN

Mary Shelley
Adapted by Robin Waterfield

Frankenstein – a tormented genius or crazed scientist?

Life has many mysteries, but there is none greater than the secret of creation. Victor Frankenstein the brilliant scientist believes he has discovered that secret and creates a life form to prove his theory. The dire and hideous consequences of this he could never have imagined, as Frankenstein's dream of life turns into a nightmare of death.

This chillingly terrifying tale is famous as one of the world's greatest horror stories. It has been retold many times in book and on film – this version is a faithful adaptation of the original Mary Shelley novel.